Samuel French Acting Edition

House on Fire

by Lyle Kessler

SAMUELFRENCH.COM   SAMUELFRENCH.CO.UK

FOR PRODUCTION ENQUIRIES

UNITED STATES AND CANADA
Info@SamuelFrench.com
1-866-598-8449

UNITED KINGDOM AND EUROPE
Plays@SamuelFrench.co.uk
020-7255-4302

Each title is subject to availability from Samuel French, depending upon country of performance. Please be aware that *HOUSE ON FIRE* may not be licensed by Samuel French in your territory. Professional and amateur producers should contact the nearest Samuel French office or licensing partner to verify availability.

MUSIC USE NOTE

IMPORTANT BILLING AND CREDIT REQUIREMENTS

HOUSE ON FIRE was originally produced in West Palm Beach, Florida, by Palm Beach Dramaworks (Producing Artistic Director, William Hayes; Managing Director, Sue Ellen Beryl) and opened on December 7, 2018. The production was directed by William Hayes, with scenic design by Bill Clarke, costume design by Brian O'Keefe, lighting design by Donald Edmund Thomas, and sound design by David Thomas. The production stage manager was Suzanne Clement Jones, and the fight choreographer was Lee Soroko. The cast was as follows:

COLMAN .... Hamish Allan-Headley
DALE..Taylor Anthony Miller
OLD MAN.. Rob Donohoe
LANE... Georgia Warner
NOAH...Christopher Kelley

The play was originally submitted in 2017 to The Dramaworkshop at Palm Beach Dramaworks.

HOUSE ON FIRE had an earlier production under the title *THE GREAT DIVIDE* at Elephant Theatre (Artistic Director, David Fofi) in Los Angeles, California on June 11, 2015. The play was directed by David Fofi and produced by Bren Coombs and Shannon McManus, with set and sound design by Elephant Stageworks, lighting design by Derrick McDaniel, and costume design by Michael Mullen. The stage managers were Dianna Leanne Wilson and Shannon Simonds, and the fight choreographer was Aaron Lyons. The cast was as follows:

COLMAN ....Adam Haas Hunter
DALE.. Brandon Bales
OLD MAN..Richard Chaves
LANE.........................Kimberly Alexander / Kate Huffman
NOAH..Mark McClain Wilson

In both productions, "Irish Lullaby" was sung by Margaret Ladd.

CHARACTERS

COLMAN

DALE

OLD MAN

LANE

NOAH

ACT ONE

Scene One

(*An old row house. Wallpaper faded, loosely hanging. Furniture worn. A bar counter. Photo of a man, woman, and two small boys on the boardwalk in Atlantic City. Another photo, unsmiling men in baseball uniforms.* The Encyclopedia of Baseball *lies nearby. Trophies hang in a cabinet, along with mitts, cleats, a catcher's mask, a Louisville Slugger, and hardballs. Books stuffed into bookcases.* **COLMAN** *stands in the doorway, wearing a backpack. He is in his early to mid-thirties. He stares past* **DALE**, *same age, at an* **OLD MAN** *lying on a couch.*)

COLMAN. Is he dead?

DALE. He's dead.

COLMAN. How can you be sure?

DALE. He's not breathing.

COLMAN. That doesn't mean he's dead.

DALE. All living things breathe, Colman.

COLMAN. All living things breathe, Dale, I'm not denying that, but this living thing might be sneaking a breath.

DALE. Sneaking a breath?

COLMAN. When you're not looking, sneaking a breath here or there.

DALE. He's dead, Colman. He's been dead for two days now.

COLMAN. How did he die, Dale? Tell me the details.

DALE. It was a night like any other night...

COLMAN. Uh-huh.

DALE. He fixed himself a ham and cheese sandwich on pumpernickel.

COLMAN. With a dab of dark mustard.

DALE. He hated the light mustard. If they brought a jar of light mustard to his table at a restaurant he would yell: *"Get this disgusting yellow shit outta my face!"*

COLMAN. That was the Old Man.

DALE. That was the Old Man, all right. He was a man of strong convictions.

COLMAN. He was a man of strong prejudices. Can we get on with the story.

DALE. He was sitting watching TV. I was in the kitchen tidying up. I heard a gurgling sound.

COLMAN. What do you mean, a gurgling sound? Can you give me an example.

DALE. No, I don't want to give you an example.

COLMAN. There are all kinds of gurgling sounds, Dale, there is a whole wide range of gurgling sounds. Am I asking too much? Dad's last sound.

DALE. All right.

COLMAN. Thank you.

DALE. It went something like this.
    (Makes gurgling sound.) Agggggggggg!

COLMAN. The Old Man would never make a sound like that.

DALE. The Old Man never died before. I dropped the dish I was washing and ran into the living room. The Old Man was lying on the couch dead.

COLMAN. He died.

DALE. He passed away...

COLMAN. The Old Man would never pass away. Croaked maybe, kicked the bucket possibly, passed away, never.

DALE. They're one and the same, Colman.

COLMAN. They're worlds apart. Pass away suggests something mellow, something sweet. The Old Man was a rotten mother fucking bastard. He would never just pass from this world to the next.

(Pause.)

DALE. Listen, you want a drink?

COLMAN. Could use a drink. Been on the road for a day and a half.

DALE. Bourbon, scotch...

COLMAN. Whatever, doesn't matter.

> *(He removes his backpack, glances around the room.)*

Home, sweet home.

DALE. *(Mixing drinks.)* Yeah, home, sweet fuckin' home.

> *(Hands COLMAN a drink.)*

To the Old Man.

COLMAN. To the fucking Old Man.

DALE. Long may he Rest in Peace.

COLMAN. The Old Man Resting in Peace! That's an oxymoron.

DALE. Whatever. To the fucking dead Old Man.

> *(Pause.)*

COLMAN. I can't drink to the fucking dead Old Man.

DALE. And why is that?

COLMAN. Because I'm not convinced. Why haven't the morticians removed the body?

DALE. I didn't want to dispose of the corpse without your say-so.

COLMAN. That's decent of you.

DALE. Embalm him, bury him, you know, et cetera...

COLMAN. No way the Old Man's gonna let anyone drain his blood, dump him into a hole in the ground.

DALE. Well, then there's always cremation.

COLMAN. The Old Man would rise up like an Avenging Angel and slay the lot of you.

DALE. He's dead, Colman. His Avenging Angel days are over.

COLMAN. He's playing possum, Dale. He's biding his time.

DALE. To what end?

COLMAN. To get me back here. To get me back in his grasp again.

DALE. That's crazy.

COLMAN. I been away ten years, Dale. I got the fuck outta Dodge.

DALE. I know.

COLMAN. He was suffocating me, he was suffocating you, he was suffocating Mom. She died an early death.

DALE. Mom died crossing the street. It was a hit-and-run.

COLMAN. She wasn't looking.

DALE. How do you know what she was doing, Colman?

COLMAN. Because he consumed her. She wasn't looking this way or that way. He was in her every thought.

DALE. What's your point?

COLMAN. She couldn't escape him, Dale. I did. It took me years to get him out of my head, my body, my arms, my legs, my cock.

DALE. Your cock?

COLMAN. So it was me fucking the li'l ladies, not him. In the beginning it was him coming not me coming. Now it's me coming. Now it's me saying, *"Look, Dad! See me! Getting it on, Dad! My dick, my balls, my fucking life!"*

DALE. I'm sorry about that, Colman.

COLMAN. An' how's life treating you, Dale?

DALE. Life's treating me just fine.

COLMAN. You got a lady?

DALE. I have a lady or two. No one special.

COLMAN. Ever bring her home?

DALE. Are you kidding?

COLMAN. Just asking.

DALE. You don't bring a Jew into a Mosque, Colman, or a Mouse into a Cat House. There is such a thing as Common Sense.

COLMAN. So now you're free to bring a li'l lady home.

DALE. I might consider it.

COLMAN. The Old Man would be all over her.

DALE. The Old Man is dead, Colman. He's lying there dead.

COLMAN. Prove it. Pinch him.

DALE. Are you serious?

COLMAN. Give him a good hard pinch.

DALE. I'm not pinching him.

COLMAN. You see? I'm making my point.

DALE. 'Cause I don't want to pinch my dead Old Man, it means he's alive?

COLMAN. Because you're afraid if you pinch your dead Old Man, he'll grab you around the neck in a chokehold.

DALE. The Old Man hasn't held me in a chokehold in years. We work the Newsstand together.

COLMAN. You and the old man are partners?

DALE. Were partners. We took turns so he could take time off.

COLMAN. And what did you do with your time off, Dale?

DALE. What do you mean, what did I do? I did things. I have a life.

COLMAN. The Old Man owns you.

DALE. I got a fucking life, Colman.

COLMAN. You exist, Dale, that's about it. Like a rock exists. Like a great big boulder exists. But you don't have a life. You just have an existence.

DALE. And what about you, Colman. What about your existence. You been on the run.

COLMAN. Call it what you will, I have a life.

DALE. Okay, good you have a life and I just exist. So be it. Let's get down to Brass Tacks now. How do you want to proceed with the funeral arrangements?

COLMAN. I'm not proceeding, Dale. He's not dead.

DALE. If I pinch him, will you be happy? Can we move along then?

COLMAN. Yeah, sure, so long you give him a good hard pinch.

DALE. I'll give him a good hard pinch.

> *(He crosses over to the **OLD MAN** lying on the couch, rolls up his sleeve.)*

Okay?

COLMAN. Okay. Go ahead.

> *(**DALE** pinches the **OLD MAN**. There is no response.)*

DALE. Satisfied?

COLMAN. No. Hardly. That was a Love Tap, Dale. Grab a chunk of his flesh an' squeeze!

> *(**DALE** grabs the **OLD MAN**'s arm, squeezes hard.)*

OLD MAN. *Ahhhhhhhhh!*

> *(The **OLD MAN** grabs **DALE** by the scruff of his neck, pulling him over the couch. **DALE** crawls across the room, gasping for breath. **COLMAN** stands watching, apprehensively.)*

(Stretching.) I'm famished. Could eat a horse. Could eat a baby elephant, trunk and all. Anyone seen a baby elephant wandering around Fishtown? How 'bout you, fella?

COLMAN. Fella?

OLD MAN. What's your name? Do I know you?

COLMAN. You know my name.

OLD MAN. You look familiar. You have a familiar ring to you. The eyes, the eyebrows, slope of the shoulder. You're not Doug Dumont, are you?

COLMAN. No, I'm not Doug Dumont.

OLD MAN. What a shame. Doug was a fine fella. Hell of a second baseman. Could field and hit the long ball. Died a few years back, eating a pizza, piece a crust got stuck in his windpipe, suffocated. Sammy's Pizza Parlor. Remember Sammy?

COLMAN. I remember Sammy.

OLD MAN. Made a hell of a pie, hard crust though. Indigestible crust. That was his downfall. You like pizza, fella? You a pizza aficionado?

COLMAN. I enjoy a good pie now and then.

(**DALE** *coughs, spits...*)

OLD MAN. What's ailing you, Dale? Had a late night?

DALE. You choked me, cut off my windpipe.

OLD MAN. Did the punishment fit the crime, Dale? Raising your hand to your own father. Pinching your dead father on his throwing arm.

DALE. You weren't dead, Dad.

OLD MAN. Well, don't make a fuckin' Federal Case outta it. We bear our pain, boys, like the Headless Horseman. You never heard him moaning and groaning 'cause he lost his head. He rode those backwoods of Sleepy Hollow like a fucking banshee. Not one fucking peep outta him.

COLMAN. It's good to see you, Dad.

OLD MAN. It's good to see you, Colman. Can you come a little closer. My eyes are not what they use to be.

COLMAN. I don't think so, Dad.

OLD MAN. And why is that?

COLMAN. I like it where I am.

OLD MAN. I don't see what's so special where you are, Colman. It's just another part of the room.

COLMAN. I'll keep my distance.

OLD MAN. You always played your cards close to the vest, remember that about you. Wanna see you up close and personal, Colman, that's all.

COLMAN. Why don't you put on your glasses then, Dad.

OLD MAN. What glasses?! You ever know me to wear glasses?

COLMAN. Well, you're older.

OLD MAN. You think the cavemen wore glasses or the Cro-Magnon Man a hearing aid?

COLMAN. Have no idea what they wore, Dad.

OLD MAN. We make do, boys. Self-reliance was the first step in what Mister Darwin called the evolutionary ladder. *Origin of the Species*. A real thriller. Nip and tuck at one time. But we beat out the Cro-Magnon Man and the Piltdown Man in the evolutionary sweepstakes. Pays to be a winner, boys.

COLMAN. You haven't changed, Dad.

OLD MAN. You got a good thing going, hold on to it. How many years has it been, Colman?

COLMAN. I haven't kept count.

OLD MAN. Well, I have, marked off every day and night like Robinson Crusoe.

COLMAN. I don't believe that, Dad.

OLD MAN. Well, then you climb the stairs and walk down the hall to my bedroom. The walls are filled with x's. Three thousand, six hundred and forty-two x's. That's how come I called for you. Had no place else to put the x's.

COLMAN. You didn't call for me, Dad. Dale said you had died.

OLD MAN. Well, you know Dale. He tends to exaggerate.

COLMAN. I stopped everything I was doing and rushed back home.

OLD MAN. Always did, even as a boy. Teacher called him a Fantasist. What does that mean? My son a Fantasist. Does that mean he dances among the daisies.

DALE. I don't dance among no daisies, Dad. I make up imaginary worlds. I've been writing while you've been away, Colman. I've written a bunch of stories.

COLMAN. What kind of stories?

DALE. Made-up worlds. Creatures who live in made-up worlds. I extrapolated.

OLD MAN. That's your problem, too much extrapolating. Too much pulling the ol' Charlie Horse.

DALE. That's masturbating, Dad, not extrapolating.

OLD MAN. One and the same.

DALE. Ahhh, Jesus, Dad.

OLD MAN. Washington Irving. Now there was a writer. *Rip Van Winkle* and *The Legend of Sleepy Hollow*. American Classics, boys. I wished I could have lived in Sleepy Hollow 'stead of fuckin' Fishtown. I think the Headless Horseman and I would have been the best of friends. What do you think, Colman?

COLMAN. I think you and that headless fella would've hit it off just fine, Dad.

OLD MAN. Do I detect a hint of sarcasm?

COLMAN. No, not at all. The Headless Horseman and you have a lot in common, Dad. I think you'd have gotten on famously.

OLD MAN. You see, this is what I missed, Colman. You're a born kibitzer, like the Old Man. Chip off the ol' fucking block. Dale here doesn't have a single, solitary Funny Bone.

DALE. I have a Funny Bone, Dad.

OLD MAN. Well, then show it to me, Dale. Where is it? Is it between the collarbone and the pelvis. At the hip joint. Where's its exact location?

DALE. I don't know its exact location. I just know it's there.

OLD MAN. Like God? Like God Almighty? I don't believe in speculation, boys, I believe in Cold Hard Facts.

COLMAN. I'd like to read your stories someday, Dale.

DALE. Well, maybe someday you can. I'll consider it, Colman.

OLD MAN. This is what I longed for, my twin boys, bonding. Last time I had these feelings was when the both of you were suckling at my breasts.

COLMAN. We suckled at Mom's breasts, Dad, not yours.

DALE. Mom breastfed us.

OLD MAN. Your mother had no milk, boys. She was as dry as an old sow. Nature did an amazing thing, though. Nature did a Darwinian thing. I took Colman to my one breast and Dale to the other. And both of you began sucking and milk flowed from my breasts, boys.

COLMAN. I'm kind of tired, Dad.

OLD MAN. I imagine you are.

COLMAN. I've been on the road for a day and a half.

OLD MAN. You've been on the road for ten years, Colman. Not a peep out of you, not a postcard. How did you find him, Dale? How did you find your long-lost brother?

COLMAN. I wasn't lost, Dad. I left. It was an Act of Will.

OLD MAN. Run away more like it. Let's call a spade a spade. It was a Coward's Retreat.

COLMAN. Whatever you say, Dad. Ran, left, vanished, skipped town...

OLD MAN. Broke my heart. Split it into a million individual pieces. Broke your sweet mother's tender heart too.

COLMAN. Mom was dead, Dad. She died years before I left.

OLD MAN. No matter. If she'd been alive her heart would've been broken. How did you find him, Dale? Did you send out a Posse?

DALE. Didn't need a Posse, Dad, posted your death online.

OLD MAN. It's a John Ford fucking World, boys. The horse and buggy to the automobile.

DALE. That wasn't John Ford, Dad. John Ford made movies. Henry Ford made automobiles.

OLD MAN. Who gives a shit. A Ford is a Ford.

COLMAN. You think I can shower now Dad, freshen up maybe, shave?

OLD MAN. A son doesn't have to ask his father for the privilege of showering. This is your house, Colman. Use it as you wish.

COLMAN. I appreciate that, Dad.

OLD MAN. So long as you don't bring 'round any of your wild floozies and desecrate the place.

COLMAN. They weren't wild floozies, Dad. They were high school students.

OLD MAN. Banging them behind the garage in a stand-up position. I know a floozy when I see a floozy.

COLMAN. I'm gonna take that shower now, Dad, use the john.

OLD MAN. Didn't even have the decency to lay 'em down. Show him the way, Dale.

COLMAN. I know the way, Dad. I lived here Once Upon a Time.

OLD MAN. An' mind that second step, it's broken. Who's working the shop by the way, Dale?

DALE. The Newsstand is closed Dad.

OLD MAN. There are daylight hours left, Dale.

DALE. There was a Death in the Family, Dad. I closed the shop out of respect.

OLD MAN. There is no fucking Death in the Family, Dale. The family is intact. Get your ass over there and take care of business. You hungry, Colman?

COLMAN. I could use a bit of grub.

OLD MAN. I'll make you my specialty, ham and cheese on pumpernickel with a dab of dark mustard. You go up take your shower. Room's made up just like the day you left it. When you come down gonna be a nice big ol' ham and cheese sandwich waiting for you.

DALE. What about me, Dad. What's going to be waiting for me when I get back from work?

OLD MAN. Maybe a slice of muenster if you're lucky, Dale.

DALE. Jesus, Dad, I have an appetite too.

OLD MAN. Just pulling the ol' proverbial leg, boy. Ham and cheese on pumpernickel be waiting for you, same as your brother. Ham and cheese better than a baby elephant, boys. Elephant fat raises the ol' Cholesterol Count worse than even Calves' Liver which is a real killer.

COLMAN. Gonna take my shower now, Dad. Use the facilities.

DALE. Gonna man the Newsstand now, Dad.

(**COLMAN** *crosses upstairs.* **DALE** *leaves.*)

OLD MAN. Family back together again. Hallelujah! God is good. I mean if there is a God, he is good.

Scene Two

(**COLMAN** *sits, eats. The* **OLD MAN** *stands behind him, watching him.*)

OLD MAN. Good, huh?

COLMAN. Delicious, Dad.

OLD MAN. You could use a little meat on the bone, Colman. Face the cold.

COLMAN. It's summer, Dad.

OLD MAN. That means winter's not far behind. "The Ant and the Grasshopper." Remember?

COLMAN. *Aesop's Fables.*

OLD MAN. Read 'em to you as a boy.

COLMAN. Loved those Fables, Dad.

OLD MAN. Grasshopper lazed in the sun all summer long, played his guitar, banged a whole host of lady grasshoppers, got his grasshopper rocks off, while the little ant had his head to the grindstone, putting away little itty-bitty pieces of food for the long cold winter to come. Remember?

COLMAN. I remember, Dad.

OLD MAN. Winter come and the little ant sat nice and cozy in his little underground chamber surrounded by thousands of itty-bitty pieces of food while Mister Grasshopper walked the Highlands, shivering and shaking, skin and bones, wasting away to nothing.

COLMAN. There's a real lesson to be learned there, Dad.

OLD MAN. Fucking Aesop. That Arab could write.

COLMAN. I thought he was Greek, Dad.

OLD MAN. Greeks stole him away from Arabia or some such place. This is why the Greek Civilization failed. When the slaves have more insights than their Masters a civilization is in its Death Throes.

COLMAN. I never considered that.

OLD MAN. The truth of the matter is it wasn't necessary for Dale to work these last three daylight hours. I just wanted to spend some Quality Time with you.

COLMAN. Quality Time?

OLD MAN. Isn't that what they call it now? Isn't that the lingo?

COLMAN. I don't know the lingo, Dad. I'm not familiar with the lingo. I don't have any children.

OLD MAN. You been away ten years, Colman. I figured you'd have at least two or three little ones by now.

COLMAN. Well, I guess you figured wrong.

OLD MAN. Moe and Joe, Penny and Liz. Wanted to see the Little Darlings.

COLMAN. Sorry to disappoint you.

OLD MAN. Well, Jesus, what kind of fornicator are you. A Man fornicates to preserve the race. He has a moral and ethical obligation.

COLMAN. I guess I'm lacking in those qualities, Dad.

OLD MAN. And if we were all lacking, boy, we would never have settled the land or become civilized beings.

COLMAN. I guess your definition of civilized beings is a whole lot different than mine.

(Pause.)

OLD MAN. I figured you'd throw the First Punch.

COLMAN. It wasn't a punch, Dad, it's just the way I feel.

OLD MAN. It was a sucker punch. You hit me below the belt before I even entered the ring.

COLMAN. This is not a ring; this is a living room.

OLD MAN. All the mighty battles of the last century happened in the Living Room. Dempsey, Tunney, Louis, Schmeling had nothing on your mom and me. The Thriller in Manilla was a Cakewalk compared to the blows your mom leveled at me.

COLMAN. You got in a few blows yourself.

OLD MAN. I never raised my hand to that woman.

COLMAN. You raised your voice. You assaulted her with verbal abuse. She died an early death.

OLD MAN. We all die an early death. Time is relative.

COLMAN. What do you want, Dad? Why did you bring me back?

OLD MAN. Well, we don't beat around the bush, do we?

COLMAN. What bush you referring to, Dad? There is no bush! You brought me back here. I wanna know why!

OLD MAN. We are a family, are we not, Colman?

COLMAN. What constitutes a family, Dad?

OLD MAN. A mother, a father and two fucking sons constitute a family.

COLMAN. A family is more than the sum of its parts, Dad.

OLD MAN. There you go again. Another sucker punch.

COLMAN. It's just my opinion.

OLD MAN. It was a fuckin' kidney punch. It was a Low Blow when the Referee wasn't looking.

COLMAN. There is no Referee, Dad.

OLD MAN. Don't kid yourself, Colman. There is always a Referee. Remember Meyer Millis?

COLMAN. Yeah, I remember Meyer Millis. He was an Umpire, Dad. He called balls and strikes for the Two-Bit League.

OLD MAN. He called more than balls and strikes. He called you Safe or Out. He was the ultimate adjudicator.

COLMAN. As I recall you weren't very happy with his adjudications. You were always in his face.

OLD MAN. He was blind as a fucking bat. Sonuvabitch, Meyer Millis. It makes my blood boil.

COLMAN. So why are you bringing him up as a Higher Authority.

OLD MAN. Well, someone has to be. Might as well be a Blind Jew. Better than a Deaf an' Dumb God.

COLMAN. We're way off the subject, Dad. You never steered a Straight Course.

OLD MAN. There is no fucking Straight Course. Life is composed of zigs and zags.

COLMAN. Why did you pretend for two whole days you were dead?

OLD MAN. To bring you home, Colman. To get your ass back in the saddle again. Satisfied?

COLMAN. *(Standing.)* No, not satisfied. Hardly satisfied.

(He starts for the stairs.)

OLD MAN. Where you going?

COLMAN. Getting my backpack. Ziggin' an' zaggin' outta here. No one's gonna shove my ass back in no saddle again!

OLD MAN. Ahh, Jesus, Colman, don't get your bowels in an uproar. You want the truth?! I'll tell you the truth!

COLMAN. *(Stopping.)* What's the truth?!

OLD MAN. This was just a Preview of Coming Attractions. Truth is that sometime in the not too distant future your Old Man will surely kick the bucket and who then is gonna attend to Dale?

COLMAN. Dale is a grown man, Dad. Dale can attend to himself.

OLD MAN. Dale is a fucking recluse. He never goes out. Dale is a head without a body. I took him into the business so he would do something, you know, have some responsibility.

COLMAN. I don't understand. Dale said he was seeing one or two different women.

OLD MAN. Only thing Dale sees are the walls of his room. Only thing he's banging away at is his computer night and day, writing.

COLMAN. Well, that's not a Bad Thing, that's a Good Thing. He's a writer.

OLD MAN. He's a writer? Who says he's a writer? Have you seen any of his writing?

COLMAN. How could I see any of his writing. I haven't been here.

OLD MAN. Nobody has seen any of his writing, God nor Man. I doubt if there is any writing.

COLMAN. That's crazy, Dad. You said yourself he's banging away at his computer all night long.

OLD MAN. You write a story, you type it up, send it off to a publication, this is the way it works. You don't lock it away in a safe at the end of the night.

COLMAN. Dale has a safe?

OLD MAN. Goddamn safe. Weighs a ton. Delivery Men could hardly get it up the stairs to his room. Broke a fucking step.

COLMAN. Jesus.

OLD MAN. I want you to read his writing. I wanna know if he is flailing away at the Abyss or if he is rising to some kind of Heavenly Bliss.

COLMAN. And what is your definition of Heavenly Bliss?

OLD MAN. Heavenly Bliss is Shakespeare, Dickens and all them Russian Mother Fuckers.

COLMAN. That's a pretty high bar you're setting.

OLD MAN. You play baseball, you don't wanna just get on base. You wanna knock it out of the park.

COLMAN. I'll read Dale's writing, if he shows it to me.

OLD MAN. If he's gonna show it to anyone, he'll show it to you. Dale needs you, Colman. He needs his brother now.

COLMAN. 'Magine he does, Dad. How could you pull the wool over his eyes like that for two whole days?

OLD MAN. You know Dale, gullibility his middle name. When he was asleep, I got up, took care a business.

(*Pause.*)

So what d'yuh say?

(*Pause.*)

COLMAN. Okay, Dad, I'll stay a while. Not indefinitely you understand.

OLD MAN. I understand.

(Pause.)

COLMAN. Anything else?

OLD MAN. What do you mean, anything else?

COLMAN. I'm asking if there is anything else you want to say to me.

OLD MAN. Well, yes, I'm sure there is. I'm sure there is a whole ream a shit I wanna say to you. But I'm tired, boy. It's not easy being dead for two whole days and then alive another. Gonna hit the sack now, need all my energy for tomorrow.

(He crosses to the stairs.)

COLMAN. What's tomorrow, Dad?

OLD MAN. Gonna drive out to Fairmount Park, the Two-Bit League. Play ball. We're together again, Colman, we're a family.

*(He climbs up the stairs. **COLMAN** stares after him.)*

Scene Three

(The morning light shines through the windows. **COLMAN,** *in shorts and a t-shirt, crosses in from the kitchen, sipping coffee.* **DALE** *enters the house, carrying a bag heavy with change. He sets it down.)*

COLMAN. Where were you, Dale?

DALE. Fell asleep at the Newsstand. Must've been exhausted.

COLMAN. 'Magine so. Staying up day and night with your dead dad.

DALE. Where is he?

COLMAN. Haven't heard a peep. Dying must've exhausted him.

(Stares at **DALE.***)*

How'd it go last night?

DALE. It was a slow night. People stopped by, offered condolences. "Sorry for your loss" kind of thing.

COLMAN. Who did they think died?

DALE. Figured it was the Old Man. I set them straight. Told them it was my Aunt Millie.

COLMAN. We have no Aunt Millie.

DALE. Well, whether we have one or not, she's dead, Colman.

COLMAN. I miss her.

DALE. You miss her?

COLMAN. I miss her already. She was a helluva lady.

DALE. She was my favorite aunt.

COLMAN. She was our only aunt.

DALE & COLMAN. Fucking Aunt Millie.

(They laugh together.)

DALE. I missed you, Colman.

COLMAN. I missed you too, Dale.

DALE. Not that much.

COLMAN. What do you mean?

DALE. You know what I mean. Use your imagination.

COLMAN. You mean because I wasn't in touch?

DALE. Something along those lines.

COLMAN. I'm sorry, Dale.

DALE. I'm sure.

COLMAN. Are you angry?

DALE. I don't know what I am. I have a whole wide range of feelings.

COLMAN. I couldn't save you, Dale. It took every ounce of energy to save myself.

DALE. I didn't need saving. I just needed communicating.

COLMAN. If I gave an inch, the Old Man'd take a mile. I was fighting for my life.

DALE. And I was fighting for mine.

COLMAN. Every inch was a milestone, every foot was a triumph.

DALE. *I needed you, Colman! I didn't know if you were alive or dead!*

COLMAN. I was alive. You knew it.

DALE. I knew it?

COLMAN. Be honest, Dale, c'mon. When you broke your foot sliding into second base, remember...

DALE. I remember.

COLMAN. I was in agony.

DALE. When you fell out of that tree...

COLMAN. I remember.

DALE. I cried all night.

>   *(Pause.)*

>   I knew you were alive. I knew you were out there. I felt your presence.

COLMAN. I missed you, Dale, swear to God.

DALE. I felt lost. I felt abandoned, Colman.

COLMAN. I was holding on for Dear Life, Dale...

DALE. Holding on to what...?

COLMAN. Myself. My being. My gonads. Had jobs in the Midwest, Ohio, then Wisconsin, Tennessee, Deep South, always on the move.

DALE. What kind of jobs?

COLMAN. Short Order Cook, dishwasher, house painter, you name it, spent time in the can, nothing serious, loitering, drinking, making a public display of myself. Life was sweet, though, life was a dream 'way from the Old Man, met a girl, met a couple women, kept moving, though, couldn't stay in one place, 'cause if I did he was always gaining...

DALE. Gaining?

COLMAN. On me. One step behind, know what I mean?

DALE. I know what you mean. He was close at hand.

COLMAN. Wouldn't let go. Couldn't shake him loose. Packed up my bags, moved to the next town. Had a breather, you know... Matter of weeks, months...

DALE. Before he showed up again.

COLMAN. Exactly. Dale...?

DALE. Yes?

COLMAN. The Old Man said you didn't have any girlfriends. He said you were making it up.

DALE. Do you believe him?

COLMAN. I don't know what to believe.

DALE. The Old Man never said a true word in his life.

COLMAN. The Old Man is a bullshit artist, I know that.

DALE. The Old Man says Blue is Green and Red is White.

COLMAN. The Old Man is a perverse sonuvabitch.

DALE. Making up shit that wasn't true. Describing a world that never was. Why did he do that?

COLMAN. To confuse us. To disorientate us. To bind us to him.

DALE. I fought, Colman.

COLMAN. You fought...?

DALE. In my own way. Different than yours. I wrote. Day and night. I have a wealth of material, locked away.

COLMAN. Locked away?

DALE. In a safe, so he couldn't touch it, couldn't get his filthy mitts on it. Hear him sometimes late at night when I'm asleep, when he imagines I'm asleep, turning the combination lock, this way and that, cursing under his breath, 'cause he can't get a grip on me, can't cubbyhole me in Time and Space, so long he can't read my writing.

COLMAN. Good for you.

DALE. He get his hands on my stories he would contaminate them, contaminate me, ruin everything.

COLMAN. You fought him.

DALE. Every word, every sentence...

COLMAN. Dale...?

DALE. Yes?

COLMAN. May I?

DALE. May you what?

COLMAN. Read a story.

(*Pause.*)

DALE. You want to read a story?

COLMAN. Yes.

DALE. One of my stories?

COLMAN. I would love to read one of your stories.

DALE. I haven't seen you in ten years, Colman, and now you want to read a story?

COLMAN. Is that so bad? Is that so terrible? I'm your brother.

DALE. You want to judge me!

COLMAN. No!

DALE. You want to judge my writing!

COLMAN. I would never judge your writing.

DALE. Is it good, is it bad? Does it rise to the occasion. Am I someone, am I somebody?

COLMAN. You are someone!

DALE. You wanna take up where the Old Man left off.

COLMAN. Dale, listen...

DALE. *The Old Man put you up to this!*

COLMAN. No! Never!

DALE. *Liar! Mother fucker!*

> *(He throws himself at* **COLMAN***, knocking him down. They wrestle on the floor. The* **OLD MAN** *appears at the top of the stairs.)*

OLD MAN. Good morning, boys. And how was your night? I slept like a baby. Slept like a Mother Fucker. Family together again.

> *(He crosses down.)*

Horsing around, huh? Boys'll be boys. Save your energy, though. Gonna take on the world today, boys, like the ol' days!

> *(He throws the mitts and the cleats at them.)*

Had all your shit lyin' 'round just in case. Man can dream can't he! *Whaddayuhsay, boys! Yuh up to it! Play ball! Play fuckin' Baseball!*

> *(He picks up his bag with all the baseball paraphernalia. He throws a ball and a mitt to* **COLMAN** *and* **DALE***. They follow him out of the house.)*

Scene Four

> *(The empty house. Early afternoon. A knock*
> *at the door. Another knock. A long moment.)*

MAN'S VOICE. *(Offstage.) Tokie! Tokie! You there, Tokie!*
We come! We're here! Fuckin' Fishtown! End of the
goddamn world! You there, Tokie! Anyone there! Rise
an' shine, li'l darlings!

GIRL'S VOICE. *(Offstage.)* I think they rised an' shined already,
Noah, it's afternoon.

NOAH. *(Offstage.)* It's just an expression, Lane. It has no
relationship to reality.

LANE. *(Peeking in window.)* Well, I'm not so keen on reality.
Tokie! Tokie! Tokie!

> *(**NOAH** appears at a side window, opens it*
> *and climbs in. He is missing an arm. **LANE***
> *climbs in behind him. She is an intense,*
> *attractive girl. They wear backpacks.)*

I don't know, Noah.

NOAH. What don't you know, Lane.

LANE. Comin' in like this.

NOAH. A Man's gotta do what a Man's gotta do.

LANE. Whaddabout a woman?

NOAH. It's all the same in the great big *Book a Life.*

LANE. I never read the great big *Book a Life.*

NOAH. Well, it's not for us to read.

LANE. I'm just saying...

NOAH. What are you saying!

LANE. We want to put our best foot forward.

NOAH. I don't have a best foot, Lane. I have two legs and
one arm. And I love my legs equally well. I don't prefer
one leg over the other.

LANE. Even so...

NOAH. *Fuck even so! I'm sick an' tired of even so!*

LANE. Let me express it another way.

NOAH. Please do.

LANE. *(Picks up photo.)* People live here. There is a family who lives here, Noah. A father, mother and two small boys. One of these boys looks just like Tokie.

NOAH. *(Stares at photo.) Sonuvabitch!* Tokie said he was alone in the world. Alone in the Universe. He never mentioned a family.

LANE. Maybe he was speaking metaphorically.

NOAH. Well, that's a language I have no interest in. I believe in particulars. I believe in the here an' now.

LANE. *(Looking around.)* The here an' now is not so bad. I like this house.

NOAH. Not a bad house. Has good bones, don'tcha think.

LANE. *(Banging wall.)* Damn good bones, Noah.

NOAH. Old houses always do. You huff an' puff at a new house and it'll fall to pieces.

LANE. That's why the Third Little Pig built his house of brick and stone.

NOAH. The Third Little Pig was one smart cookie.

LANE. He was my favorite Little Pig.

NOAH. Well, he was the only surviving pig, wasn't he? Big Bad Wolf ate the two other little pigs, stupid dumb pigs who built their homes of straw and hay.

LANE. They learned their lesson.

NOAH. Fucking lesson. They were two dead little pigs.

LANE. It's a sad story.

NOAH. Sad so much as the Third Pig lost his two little brother pigs, I'll grant you that. That part of the story is indeed tragic. But in the end he disposed of the Big Bad Wolf who shimmied down the chimney and burned to death in a pot of boiling water.

LANE. I love that third little pig.

NOAH. Well, let's not get carried away, Lane. He's just a fuckin' pork chop after all.

LANE. He was more than that.

NOAH. Mister Oink, Oink Pork Chop, composed of ham hocks and pigs' feet and strips of fucking bacon.

LANE. You ruin everything.

NOAH. Reality is a Sorry Business.

LANE. I can only take so much reality.

NOAH. I understand that.

LANE. I prefer flights of fancy.

NOAH. Well, flights of fancy aren't going to put any food on the table.

LANE. I need to take a shower, freshen up and chow down.

NOAH. In that order?

LANE. In any order. I'm not big on order. *Listen!*

NOAH. What?

LANE. You hear it?

NOAH. I hear nothing.

LANE. A woman singing, far away.

NOAH. What's she singing?

LANE. *(In an Irish accent.)*
OVER IN KILLARNEY,
MANY YEARS AGO,
ME MITHER SANG A SONG TO ME
IN TONES SO SWEET AND LOW.

NOAH. I'll say this 'bout you, Lane... You have fucking hearing.

LANE. Always did, even as a little girl.

NOAH. You can hear things no other mortal can hear.

LANE. Can hear the wings of a butterfly, can hear a child crying miles away. Once I thought, I imagined, I heard the Voice of God.

NOAH. I don't wanna go there. Life is short an' time is fleetin'. You explore upstairs and I'll get the Lay of the Land downstairs an' we'll compare notes.

LANE. Okay.

NOAH. Okay.

*(**LANE** crosses upstairs. **NOAH** opens drawers.)*

LANE. *(Offstage.)* Noah!

NOAH. Yes.

LANE. *(Offstage.)* Jesus Christ, Noah! You gotta see this!

NOAH. What is it?

LANE. *(Offstage.)* A room covered with x's. The walls and ceilings covered with thousands of x's. Come on up.

NOAH. I'm not particularly interested in seeing a room full of x's.

LANE. *(Offstage.)* I'm talking big x's, little x's, teeny-weeny little x's and huge gargantuan x's.

NOAH. Don't give a good goddamn the size of the x's. Not interested in x's.

LANE. *(Crosses down.)* It's mystical, Noah. This is a holy place.

NOAH. Nothing mystical about x's. A fucking illiterate can make an x.

LANE. There's a message on those walls. They're saying something holy.

NOAH. Yeah, like x marks the spot.

LANE. That's not funny, Noah. Why must you denigrate everything.

NOAH. It's my Nature, Lane. Don't take it personally.

LANE. I'm tired, Noah. It's been a long trip.

NOAH. Why don't you lie down in that Holy Room and get some z's, Lane. Meantime I'll give the house a Once-Over.

LANE. If you don't mind, I'll lie down in one of the other rooms.

NOAH. Lie down wherever you wish, Lane. I'll keep an eye out.

(**LANE** *crosses off. A moment. She crosses back.*)

LANE. Noah...

NOAH. Yes.

LANE. *(Crossing down.)* In the other room...

NOAH. More x's?

LANE. No x's. A safe.

NOAH. A safe? What's inside?

LANE. Something precious, I imagine. I'm shocked. I thought Tokie was on the up and up.

NOAH. Life is a series of disappointments. What can I say.

LANE. We've been candid with him.

NOAH. We never held anything back.

LANE. You've given him so much.

NOAH. I gave him the shirt off my back.

LANE. He was wearing it when he left.

NOAH. What was ours was his.

LANE. But not vice versa, obviously. He said he had nothing. He said he was destitute.

NOAH. Destitute my long-lost fuckin' arm. No wonder he run away. Keeping all those hidden riches away from us.

LANE. *(Sits on couch.)* I'm tired, I'm so tired, Noah.

NOAH. Why don'tcha get some shut-eye, Lane. Meantime I'll pry open that sucker.

LANE. It's solid steel, Noah. I'm afraid it's impenetrable.

NOAH. Nothin's impenetrable. It's the First Law of Physics. If the Mysteries of Nature can be unlocked one at a time, this safe should be Easy Pickin's. You get some sleep, Lane, I'll tend to that safe

> *(**LANE** lies down on the couch. **NOAH** covers her with a blanket. He climbs the stairs.)*

LANE.

> OVER IN KILLARNEY,
> MANY YEARS AGO,
> ME MITHER SANG A SONG TO ME
> IN TONES SO SWEET AND LOW.

> *(Her voice trails off, she is asleep. Sound of hammering coming from Dale's room upstairs.)*
>
> *(Blackout.)*

Scene Five

(Later. **LANE** *asleep on the couch. The sound of hammering from Dale's room. Sound of a car pulling up.)*

OLD MAN. *(Offstage.)* What...? What...? What is it we do? What is it we did?

DALE. *(Offstage.)* We played ball, Dad. We played baseball.

OLD MAN. *(Offstage.)* And what is baseball?

COLMAN. *(Offstage.)* Baseball is a sport.

OLD MAN. *(Offstage.)* But not the Sport of Kings. Not the Sport of the Nobility.

> (**NOAH** *peeks out upstairs.* **LANE** *hides behind the couch. The* **OLD MAN,** **DALE,** *and* **COLMAN** *enter, wearing cleats and carrying baseball gear.)*

Baseball is the sport of what...? Someone? Anyone?

DALE. Baseball is the sport of the Common Ordinary Man.

OLD MAN. Exactly. You know your history, Dale, gotta hand it to you. And who invented baseball?

COLMAN. Abner Doubleday.

OLD MAN. Abner fuckin' Doubleday. A true American hero. Forget Washington. Forget Lincoln. Forget Paul Revere. Forget the fuckin' Forefathers. Abner Doubleday invented the Great American Pastime. Which is...? Which is...? Someone? Anyone? Which is...?

DALE. Baseball.

OLD MAN. Fuckin' baseball. Did you see me, boys? Did you see your Old Man out on the Mound today throwing Aces?!

COLMAN. They couldn't touch you.

OLD MAN. Screwball, Fastball, Change a Pacer, keep 'em guessing, boys, is my motto.

DALE. It's a good motto, Dad.

OLD MAN. Don't echo me, boy. Say something new.

DALE. Meyer Millis.

OLD MAN. Don't speak that man's name in my house!

COLMAN. You were robbed, Dad.

OLD MAN. I was more than robbed, I was raped and sodomized.

DALE. You were pitching a Perfect Game.

COLMAN. It was a terrible call, Dad.

DALE. It was the worse call in the History of Baseball. That man was out by a mile.

OLD MAN. I would've tarred and feathered the bastard if there was any tar and feathers around.

DALE. You did worse, Dad.

OLD MAN. I called him every name in the book.

COLMAN. And some not even in the book.

DALE. I wasn't referring to the names. You broke his arm.

OLD MAN. I doubt that.

DALE. It was hanging from his shoulder.

OLD MAN. That's what arms do, Dale. They hang from shoulders.

DALE. He was screaming in pain.

OLD MAN. He raised his hand to me.

COLMAN. He raised his hand to eject you from the game.

OLD MAN. How would I know that? I'm not a Mind Reader. I'm an Albanian, boys. We react to a raised hand. Albanians don't take any shit. It's our Heritage.

DALE. You told us, Dad.

OLD MAN. Well, then I'll tell you again. Albanians never lost a war, 'cause no one nor nobody would dare invade our soil. Albanians don't need guns or planes or mustard gas to ward off the enemy, don't need Weapons of Mass Destruction. 'Cause we have our hands. Look at these hands, boys. What are these hands?

DALE. Albanian hands, Dad.

OLD MAN. Fuckin' A, Albanian. They'll choke the life outta anyone who invades our soil. What are we, boys? Who are we?

COLMAN. Albanians, Dad.

NOAH. *(Upstairs.)* You never told us you were an Albanian, Tokie.

OLD MAN. *(Startled.) What the fuck...*

NOAH. I thought you were a red-blooded American Boy, and now I discover you're a fuckin' Albanian.

OLD MAN. *Who the fuck are you? How did you get in here?*

NOAH. We come a long way, Tokie. We come across the Great Divide. Isn't that true, Lane?

LANE. *(Comes out.)* It's true, Tokie. We come looking for you across the Great Colossal Divide.

OLD MAN. Another one! They're all over the place!

NOAH. Tokie... Tokie... Tokie...

LANE. Tokie...

OLD MAN. Who are they talking to? Who the hell is Tokie?

NOAH. Tell him, Tokie. Tell him who you are.

COLMAN. It's me, Dad. It's my nickname. I'm Tokie.

OLD MAN. You're not no fuckin' Tokie, you're Colman! I named you!

NOAH. Well, that's the problem.

LANE. That's the problem right there in a nutshell.

NOAH. We don't believe in Given Names.

LANE. We're ideologically opposed to Given Names!

OLD MAN. Where am I? What Rabbit Hole have I fallen into! Who is that fuckin' one-armed freak?

NOAH. Your Old Man has a mouth on him.

OLD MAN. What rock did they crawl out from under.

NOAH. Tell him who we are, Tokie. Introduce us.

COLMAN. That's Noah. And the girl is Lane. They're my acquaintances.

LANE. Pleased to meet you.

NOAH. Pleased to make your acquaintance.

OLD MAN. *Fuck you!* How did they get in here? Did you give them a key?

COLMAN. I don't have a key, Dad. I threw away my key years ago.

OLD MAN. *How did they get in my house?!*

NOAH. Through the window.

OLD MAN. You broke in?

NOAH. We were tired. We came a long way.

LANE. We came across the Great Divide.

OLD MAN. I want them out of here, Colman. Tell them to leave.

NOAH. You never told us you had an Old Man, Tokie. Or a brother. Is this your brother?

DALE. I'm Dale. Pleased to meet you.

> *(He crosses toward them, hand outstretched. The* **OLD MAN** *stops him.)*

OLD MAN. Are you crazy? Are you fuckin' outta your mind? Offering them your hand!

DALE. What else could I offer?

OLD MAN. You lack discretion, Dale. Common sense. This is no fuckin' Meet an' Greet. These are intruders. I want them outta here!

NOAH. We'll leave, Old Man.

LANE. We'll definitely leave.

NOAH. After we get what we came for.

OLD MAN. And what did you come for?

NOAH. We came for Tokie.

LANE. Tokie left us.

NOAH. High an' dry.

COLMAN. I'm sorry, Noah.

NOAH. You're sorry? Sorry? After what I gave you. After how I opened up my heart to you.

LANE. What was ours was yours.

NOAH. All the work, all my dedication. I picked you up off the street. You were nothing, you were nobody.

LANE. You were lying in your own piss.

OLD MAN. Is this true? Are they speaking the truth?

COLMAN. It's true, Dad. I fell on some hard times.

NOAH. We gave him a life.

LANE. We gave him a livelihood.

OLD MAN. What was your livelihood?

COLMAN. This is not the Time or Place, Dad.

NOAH. Left us an' never looked back.

LANE. Left us in the Dead of Night. Woke up in the morning, spot next to me on the bed was empty. Called out his name, called "Tokie!" "Tokie!"

NOAH. I came running.

LANE. Couldn't believe it. Couldn't believe he would desert us like that.

NOAH. Caused me genuine anguish to see my sister's grief.

DALE. Lane's your sister?

NOAH. Born an' bred.

DALE. How did you find him?

OLD MAN. Don't ask 'em fuckin' questions.

LANE. Saw his license. Memorized the address. Memorized everything about Tokie. His eyes, his nose, the slope of his chin...

COLMAN. Why don't we leave now, Noah. I'll explain everything later.

NOAH. Oh, we'll leave all right, soon as we get the goodies.

COLMAN. What goodies?

NOAH. Goodies hidden away in the safe upstairs.

COLMAN. There are no goodies upstairs. Just a bunch of stories.

NOAH. You must think I'm wet behind the ears. No one locks stories up in a safe. What's the combination?

COLMAN. I don't know the combination.

NOAH. Well, who does. Give me the combination, Old Man.

OLD MAN. No.

(**NOAH** *crosses to the* **OLD MAN.**)

NOAH. Warnin' yuh. Give me the combination or I'll hurt you.

DALE. He doesn't know the combination. I'm the only one knows it. But I'll never give it to you. Never give it to no one.

NOAH. *(Stares at him.)* I don't know about that.

COLMAN. He'll never give it to you, Noah. God is my witness. They're just stories.

DALE. You can kill me and I still won't give it.

NOAH. 'Magine that's true. But whaddabout Tokie, suppose I kill him. Will that change your mind?

> *(He crosses to* **COLMAN**, *kicks his legs out from under him.)*

Gonna count to ten and then blow out his brains.

> *(He takes out his gun, presses it against* **COLMAN**'s *head.)*

One, two, three, four...

LANE. *Noah!*

NOAH. Shut up, Lane, I'm counting.

LANE. I'm pregnant!

NOAH. What?

LANE. I said I'm pregnant. Tokie's baby. Baby needs a daddy. Someone to hold him and rock him and protect him from the world. World's a Dark Place, Noah. Baby needs his daddy to show him the Light.

> *(***NOAH** *stares at* **LANE**. *Everyone else stares at her.)*
>
> *(Blackout.)*

ACT TWO

Scene One

(A moment later. **NOAH** *moves away from* **COLMAN**, *pockets his gun.* **LANE** *speaks.)*

LANE. May I tell you about the baby? My baby, our baby, God's baby.

OLD MAN. Yes, please do, please tell us about the baby.

LANE. Such a sweet baby, such a glorious baby, such a handsome baby.

OLD MAN. Well, he would be handsome, he's my grandson.

(COLMAN stands, cautiously.)

LANE. I can hear him. I hear his voice.

DALE. How is that possible?

NOAH. Lane hears things. She was born with a gift.

LANE. I can hear the fish in the sea, honest to God, I can hear an elephant moving through the African brush. I can hear the Angels sing.

OLD MAN. Well, that's a little far-fetched.

LANE. No, no, no, Angels sing, there's a Heavenly Choir.

NOAH. When I was a li'l boy I would wake up and hear Lane singing along with them. It was a song like no other song. It helped me through the Hard Times.

LANE. I'm sorry for the Hard Times, Noah.

NOAH. I'm not complaining mind you, we play the hand we're dealt.

LANE. Yes, but you were dealt cards from the bottom of the deck.

NOAH. I'm just saying you were my Saving Grace, Lane.

OLD MAN. This is all very sweet and tender but I do wanna hear about the baby.

LANE. He has a wonderful voice, he has a melodic voice. He is very curious about things. Where we came from, where we're going. He has a Natural Curiosity.

DALE. I like him already.

OLD MAN. Can we get on with the story. Can we stop the interruptions.

LANE. He has acute hearing. He takes after me in that respect. And he has a tough-mindedness like his father and his grandfather, like the Old Man.

OLD MAN. Thank you.

LANE. Women will love him, men adore him, children idolize him. He will go on to achieve greatness.

COLMAN. What makes you think you're pregnant?

LANE. I have Morning Sickness.

COLMAN. It might be something you ate.

LANE. I feel him in me, Tokie. I feel his presence.

COLMAN. I'm only saying...

LANE. I know what you're saying. I get the implication.

COLMAN. Why didn't you say something?

LANE. I was gonna say something. I was intending to tell you the very morning that you disappeared.

OLD MAN. This is all Water under the Bridge. We are now all one extended family, bound together by this baby, by this child who will go on to greatness.

LANE. I love your Old Man. I love everything about him.

OLD MAN. Break out the crystal, Dale. We'll have a toast.

DALE. We haven't used the crystal since Mom died.

OLD MAN. I was waiting for just such an occasion. I knew you had it in you, Colman, through the years, the long years, the lean years...

COLMAN. Had what in me, Dad?

OLD MAN. The potential...

COLMAN. What potential?

OLD MAN. To marry, settle down, raise a family.

COLMAN. Those were not my intentions, Dad. They've never been my intentions.

LANE. I was so happy for a moment and now I'm so sad.

OLD MAN. I'm surprised at you, Colman, really.

COLMAN. What should I do, Dad? Should I lie?

OLD MAN. Yes, yes, you should lie. Lies are a good thing if they keep everyone happy. And then sometimes if you're lucky, if you were born under the right star, sometimes the lie becomes the truth.

COLMAN. This is pure bullshit, Dad.

OLD MAN. This is the truest thing I've ever said, Colman. People who proclaim the truth are speaking a lie. A lie lurks under every truth. A lie is just sitting there biding its time waiting to emerge triumphant. I'll take a Liar every time over a Truth-Teller.

NOAH. I like your Old Man. He's a wise Old Man.

COLMAN. Ahhh, Jesus...

OLD MAN. I appreciate that. I've had little or no recognition in my time.

NOAH. I wish I had an Old Man like you. My whole life would've been different. I wouldn't be standing here with a missing arm.

OLD MAN. I'm sorry for your lost arm. I grieve for your lost arm.

NOAH. You grieve for it?

OLD MAN. A man loses an arm, a man loses a piece of himself which cannot be reclaimed. Tell us how you lost your arm, Noah.

NOAH. No, no, I don't wanna muddy the occasion. This is a happy occasion.

OLD MAN. You won't muddy it, you will in fact deepen it. What is joy without sorrow.

NOAH. I feel so at home here. I feel like I've finally found a place.

COLMAN. Dad, please...

OLD MAN. Hush, Colman, not now. Tell us the story, Noah, while Dale is breaking out his mother's crystal.

NOAH. I never had an Old Man, I had an Old Lady.

LANE. A terrible Old Lady, worse than any Old Man.

NOAH. We'll skip the Early Years, the formative years, we'll get right to the Heart of the Matter.

OLD MAN. Yes, yes, get to the heart...

NOAH. Scraped by, what the fuck, days in, days out. A lifetime of days. And then what. What did it add up to the Days of my Life.

LANE. You don't have to go into this, Noah. It's not necessary.

NOAH. It is necessary, Lane. I need to say it, I need to spell it out. She called me "Good for Nothing." My own mother, the Old Lady, called me a "Good for Nothing."

OLD MAN. Good for Nothing?

NOAH. Morning, noon an' night. Drunk or sober. The same words, the same inflection. *"Good for Nothing."* Cut right through me. "Good for fuckin' Nothing"!

OLD MAN. This is terrible.

NOAH. I could've been somebody. Instead became a "Good for Nothing"!

LANE. No, no, you were never a "Good for Nothing."

NOAH. Let me tell the story, Lane, as I see it, as I lived it...

LANE. Go ahead, Noah, I'm sorry.

NOAH. Stole from the rich, stole from the poor, was never discriminating. Looked after my sister, though, sent money home.

LANE. It made all the difference.

NOAH. She called me up told me the Old Lady was dying, asked to see me one last time. I was working at Bob's Big Boy at the time, had rehabilitated myself, twisted and turned my psyche outta my natural inclination to rob an' steal an' beat an' maim into a nine-to-fiver, honest to God, Bob's fuckin' Big Boy.

DALE. That must've taken some doing.

NOAH. Discipline and fortitude and an enormous will to be something better. Rushed home to pay my respects. "Mom," I said, "Mom... It's me, it's Noah." She stared straight through me as if I wasn't there, and then I saw it, the flicker, the sudden illumination, intelligence returning. And then she said it, she said the words...

LANE. No, no, don't say it, Noah, it's not necessary.

NOAH. I need to say it, I wanna say it, Lane. *"Good for Nothing. Good for fuckin' Nothing!"* I left the Nursing Home in a daze, stole the first car I come across, sped away mile-a-minute, lost control, slammed into a tree, severed an arm, lost an arm, woke up left arm was gone. Bye bye Birdie.

OLD MAN. I grieve for that arm. I grieve for that Birdie.

NOAH. I appreciate that, Old Man. It makes all the difference in the world to me.

DALE. The crystal is all broke out now, Dad. Should I pour?

OLD MAN. Yes, yes, let's drink to Good Times, to Better Times. Let's leave all the shit behind.

COLMAN. We can't leave all the shit behind, Dad. The shit is right here with us, now, staring us in the face...

OLD MAN. Well, then I'll drink to leaving some of the shit behind. Life can and will be beautiful.

LANE. I like that sentiment.

OLD MAN. There are so many toasts. Pour the bourbon, pour the scotch, pour the vodka. Let's get on with it.

> (**DALE** *pours liquor in each of the crystal glasses.*)

NOAH. I would like to make the first toast to my sister, Lane, who I have loved and cherished and cared for all the years of our lives. And without whose love and devotion I would be dead an' gone these many years.

LANE. And I wish to toast my brother, Noah, who in spite of his physical limitations and the abuse he has suffered over the years from his demented Old Lady and his teachers and counselors and the police and the

court-appointed attorneys, and the terrible, ancient
Penal System, has still managed to watch over me and
protect me and keep me outta harm's way.

DALE. And I wish to toast my brother, Colman, who is also
referred to as Tokie and my new sister-in-law, Lane and
her brother Noah and the little baby who is on his way.

OLD MAN. Yes, yes, let's toast the baby, a dream come true,
my grandchild. If only my wife were here to share in
my joy. Can you believe it. First I was dead for two days
and then I was alive, a fucking miracle in and of itself,
and now I am about to become a grandfather. Miracles
abide in this terrible place called Fishtown on the edge
of the Delaware River, home of killers and robbers and
four-flushers. A baby is coming into the world. My
baby. My baby boy.

COLMAN. Not your baby boy, Dad, my baby boy.

OLD MAN. Whatever. Whoever. Let's not quibble. A baby
boy.

> *(He raises his glass.* **NOAH, LANE,** *and* **DALE**
> *raise their glasses, drink.* **COLMAN** *sits there,*
> *glaring, apprehensively.)*

Scene Two

(Dawn. The early morning light peeks through the blinds. **LANE** *asleep on the couch.* **COLMAN** *crosses down the stairs, carrying his backpack. He tip-toes across the living room.* **LANE** *wakes.)*

LANE. Tokie!

*(***COLMAN*** hides the backpack.)*

You going somewhere?

COLMAN. I was gonna take a walk, get a breath of fresh air.

LANE. I could use a breath a fresh air myself.

(She puts on her shoes.)

COLMAN. What is it you want, Lane?

LANE. I'm not sure what you're asking.

COLMAN. With me, with my family.

LANE. I don't want nothing with you or your family.

COLMAN. Then why are you here?

LANE. I thought you loved me.

COLMAN. I never said I loved you.

LANE. Action speaks louder than words.

COLMAN. What's that suppose to mean?

LANE. You were inside me.

COLMAN. Yes, I was inside you.

LANE. You came inside me.

COLMAN. Does that mean I love you?

LANE. You cried out in pleasure.

COLMAN. This is all true.

LANE. You held me tightly.

COLMAN. I never said I loved you.

LANE. I thought you did.

COLMAN. I have no control over your thoughts.

LANE. When you were inside me, holding me tightly, clinging to me with every ounce of your being, I imagined I was being loved.

COLMAN. I'm sorry about that.

LANE. And then I woke up and turned over and you were gone.

COLMAN. I'm so sorry.

LANE. And I had this thing inside me, this live thing, this sprout.

COLMAN. A sprout?

LANE. Growing inside me, this child who was of you and of me.

COLMAN. How do you know?

LANE. I told you I know. A woman knows.

COLMAN. Have you seen a doctor?

LANE. Yes, I've seen a doctor.

COLMAN. What doctor have you seen?

LANE. I've seen Doctor Bob.

COLMAN. Doctor Bob? You're kidding me.

LANE. I spoke with Doctor Bob.

COLMAN. Doctor Bob is not a doctor. Doctor Bob is a Bookie. He's a Numbers Runner.

LANE. They call him Doctor.

COLMAN. This is bullshit.

LANE. It isn't.

COLMAN. This is fucking bullshit.

LANE. I'm pregnant!

COLMAN. Then come with me tomorrow. I'll make an appointment.

LANE. An appointment with who?

COLMAN. A real doctor, a legitimate doctor, who can do a blood test to determine if you are pregnant or not.

LANE. And will that make you happy?

COLMAN. Will what make me happy?

LANE. When you discover I am really pregnant. Will you be happy?

COLMAN. You are not pregnant.

LANE. But on the off chance that I am, on the infinitesimally small chance that I am actually pregnant, will you be happy?

> *(Pause.)*

> *Tokie?*

COLMAN. I don't know what I will be.

LANE. You don't want the baby, isn't that true?

COLMAN. There is no baby!

LANE. But if there is one, what then?

COLMAN. *There is no fucking baby!*

> *(LANE begins to cry.)*

> Lane?

> *(LANE shakes her head.)*

> I'm sorry, Lane.

LANE. Why don't you just go, Tokie, get some air.

COLMAN. I didn't mean to hurt you.

LANE. I have your baby inside me and you don't love me and that hurts, that's what hurts.

COLMAN. I'm making an appointment first thing tomorrow, find out the truth.

LANE. There is no truth, didn't you hear your wise Old Man. Even a truth is a lie. There is a baby inside me, growing inside me, that's the truth and that's also a lie and it doesn't matter.

COLMAN. I need some fresh air, Lane. I need a drink.

LANE. Yes, go, please, have a drink…

> *(COLMAN stares at LANE a long moment, turns, crosses out of the house. LANE sits there, crying. DALE appears at the top of the stairs, crosses down.)*

DALE. I believe you.

LANE. *(Looking up.)* You believe me?

DALE. I'm a light sleeper, heard you arguing.

LANE. We weren't arguing.

DALE. What were you doing?

LANE. I don't know what we were doing. I don't have a name for it. All I know is that I hurt so badly.

DALE. I'm so sorry.

LANE. I thought he would be happy. I thought he would be overjoyed at the news.

DALE. I would be.

LANE. You would be?

DALE. If it was my baby, I would be more than overjoyed.

LANE. It couldn't be your baby because we never were intimate.

DALE. I understand.

LANE. We never so much as touched.

DALE. I'm extrapolating, that's what writers do.

LANE. I don't know much about extrapolating.

DALE. I can teach you.

LANE. You can teach me how to extrapolate?

DALE. It's a wonderful thing. It gives you the freedom not to be in your own skin.

LANE. Whose skin can you be in?

DALE. It doesn't matter. Whoever you want. Is there anybody?

LANE. Yes, there is one person.

DALE. And who might that be?

LANE. Sonja Henie. She was an ice skater, a figure skater, an Olympic Champion. My father adored her.

DALE. I never heard of her.

LANE. She was way before our time or even his time, really. He idolized her as a boy. She was a movie star. He watched her old movies on late-night TV.

DALE. Did your father ice skate?

LANE. Night and day. He had a wonderful grace. I was terrible on the ice. I couldn't keep my balance. I was no Sonja Henie.

DALE. Well, who is?

LANE. That's true. Who is! On second thought, I don't wanna be no Sonja Henie. She was just a bitch on ice.

DALE. That was a fast transformation.

LANE. I'm like that, one moment I'm passionate about one thing, another moment, something else. I don't wanna spend my nights and days on no Ice Skating Rink.

DALE. You were close to your dad.

LANE. For the first few years, then he drifted away. I search for him in every Ice Skating Rink in every city we travel to.

(**DALE** *is lacing his shoes.*)

You going somewhere?

DALE. Going to work.

LANE. What do you do?

DALE. I work at a Newsstand in the day. At night I write stories.

LANE. What kind of stories?

DALE. All kinds of stories.

LANE. Can you be more specific.

DALE. Fables. Tales actually. Imaginary worlds.

LANE. Oh. I could tell you were someone special when we first met.

DALE. You could?

LANE. I had a feelin'. An' I trust my feelin's.

DALE. I trust my feelin's too. My feelin's never ever betray me.

LANE. I feel the same way. When everything else is lost and gone, there are always one's feelin's.

DALE. To cling to.

LANE. To hold on to.

DALE. To give us strength and courage.

LANE. To help us...

DALE. ...Through the night.

(*Pause.*)

LANE. Well...

DALE. Well...

> *(Pause.)*

I gotta go now.

LANE. Yes, of course. Have a good day.

DALE. Thank you. I'll try. You too.

> *(He crosses out of the house.* **NOAH** *crosses in from the kitchen.)*

NOAH. That was sweet.

LANE. Noah!

NOAH. Sweet an' tender.

LANE. Whaddayuh doin' here? Where'd yuh come from?

NOAH. Out back. Couldn't sleep, hadda splittin' headache. Walked it off. Cleared my head.

LANE. You get those migraines.

NOAH. Tension builds up. Took a walk. Fuckin' Fishtown. Not one single, solitary fish out there.

LANE. You're kidding.

NOAH. Kid yuh not. Place called Fishtown. Where are the goddamn fish!

LANE. There are no buffalo in Buffalo, Noah.

NOAH. You makin' a point...

LANE. I'm just sayin'...

NOAH. I know what you're sayin', I'm doin' the sayin'. No fish in Fishtown, just people. All kinds a people, some good, some bad. You remember how I dealt with bad people.

LANE. In the Ol' Days you would come home black an' blue. I tended your wounds.

NOAH. In the Ol' Days I had two good arms an' two good roarin' fists. Now I only have one good arm an' one good roarin' fist.

LANE. *(Takes his hand.)* But it's a great big roarin' fist, Noah. An' the way I see it, it only takes one great roarin' fist to put an end to any argument.

NOAH. That's exactly the way I see it.

LANE. Some of those fellas meant you no harm, though.

NOAH. Those are the worse kind.

LANE. Why is that, Noah?

NOAH. Because there are no "mean you no harm" sonsuvbitches out there. I've been telling you this for years, Lane, trying to educate you, but it comes to no avail.

LANE. It comes to an avail, Noah. I hear you.

NOAH. You have a big heart, Lane, an' the bigger the heart, the more likely it is to get hurt.

LANE. I can fend for myself, Noah.

NOAH. If that's the case whyjuh tell 'em you were pregnant?

LANE. 'Cause I am pregnant.

NOAH. Lane...?

LANE. I'm fuckin' pregnant, Noah.

NOAH. *(Softly.)* You have no uterus, Lane.

LANE. I have a uterus. I have a goddamn uterus.

NOAH. You had an infection when you were a young girl. The doctor removed your uterus.

LANE. The doctor removed my fibroids. I had extensive fibroids.

NOAH. The doctor removed your fibroids along with your uterus.

LANE. The doctor left a piece of my uterus, enough of a piece for a tiny itty-bitty cell to cling to an' grow an' develop into a strong, healthy baby.

NOAH. We've been through this before, Lane. I don't want you to get hurt. I don't want you to be disappointed.

LANE. Don't do this to me, Noah! Don't take away my dreams!

NOAH. I wouldn't. I couldn't.

LANE. *I want this baby. I need this baby. I am attached to this baby.*

NOAH. Okay, it's okay, Lane, let's forget I ever mentioned it.

(**LANE** *calms down.*)

Let's move on.

LANE. Move on to where...?

NOAH. I need something.

LANE. What do you need?

NOAH. This is important, Lane. You listenin'?!

LANE. I'm listening.

NOAH. There's money in this house, Lane, I smell the stench a it. The Old Man doesn't believe in banks or IRA Accounts, he is a rugged individualist, maybe the last of the breed.

LANE. What is it you need, Noah?

NOAH. If you can hear the wings of a butterfly, you can certainly hear the tumblers inside that safe.

LANE. There are only stories in that safe, Noah. Dale's stories.

NOAH. Don't be so fuckin' naive, Lane. Who locks up stories in a safe. The Old Man's been squirrelin' away money over the years. Thirty, forty years of nickels an' dimes add up.

LANE. That safe is solid steel, Noah.

NOAH. All you gotta do is press your ear to the door, Lane, turn the tumbler one way an' then another. Listen for the click, that's all it takes.

LANE. I don't know.

NOAH. What don'tcha know, Lane! One click, two clicks, three clicks. You don't want blood to be shed, do yuh?

LANE. No, I don't want blood to be shed.

NOAH. We can do this the Easy Way or the Hard Way, Lane.

LANE. I don't want the Hard Way, Noah. I've seen the Hard Way.

NOAH. It's in your hands then, Lane.

LANE. Let's do it the Easy Way, then.

NOAH. Okay, then. Good thinking, Lane.

LANE. I'll press my ear to the safe, Noah, I'll turn the tumbler one way an' then another, I'll listen for the clicks.

NOAH. You do that, Lane. However long it takes.

(**LANE** *climbs the stairs.* **NOAH** *lights a cigarette, smokes. The* **OLD MAN** *enters, carrying groceries.*)

OLD MAN. Terrible addiction, tobacco, Noah. You lost one arm already, don't wanna lose another.

NOAH. From smokin'?

OLD MAN. From anything harmful to the system. Drink a glass of hot water with a slice of lemon every morning of my life. Secret of my strength and stamina.

NOAH. Is that a fact.

OLD MAN. Same as my Old Man and his Old Man before him. Granddad lived to be a hundred and thirty-six. Broke the record.

NOAH. What record? World record?

OLD MAN. No, Albanian record. Don't know 'bout the world. Fella could be livin' somewhere in Tibet, somewhere high up in the Himalayas, a hundred an' eighty, hundred an' ninety years of age.

NOAH. It's a possibility.

OLD MAN. Air is paper-thin up there, people develop a greater lung capacity. Not like down here in Fishtown. Every breath you take might be the last.

NOAH. *(Puts out cigarette.)* Dangerous place.

(*The* **OLD MAN** *sits opposite* **NOAH**, *studies him.*)

OLD MAN. You ever play ball?

NOAH. Baseball?

OLD MAN. What other ball is there.

NOAH. I played ball in the Ol' Days, in the long-gone Olden Days.

OLD MAN. When you had two hands and two arms.

NOAH. Yeah, when I was what you would call intact.

OLD MAN. I bet you were a helluva Ball Player.

NOAH. I got on base.

OLD MAN. What position did you play?

NOAH. I pitched. Had a helluva fastball.

OLD MAN. How fast is fast?

NOAH. Never clocked it. Fast enough, though. No one could touch it.

OLD MAN. Which arm did you lose? Not your pitching arm, I hope.

NOAH. No, not my pitching arm, the other arm.

OLD MAN. Well, then you could still pitch.

NOAH. Well, yes, theoretically.

OLD MAN. No, not theoretically, practically. You can still throw a ball past Home Plate.

NOAH. Yes, I can do that if push came to shove.

OLD MAN. Well, push has come to shove. You ever hear of Hugh Ignatius Daily?

NOAH. 'Fraid not. Name doesn't ring a bell.

OLD MAN. He was a one-armed pitcher, played for Cleveland. We're talkin' Ancient History now, Legendary Shit. Hugh Ignatius Daily threw a no-hit, no-run game against Philadelphia.

NOAH. How is that possible.

OLD MAN. I shit you not.

(*Picks up the large book from the bar.*)

Encyclopedia of Baseball. My Bible. Look 'im up!

(*Hands it to* **NOAH.**)

Hugh Ignatius Daily. Spelled D.A.I.L.Y. They say he threw a ball with his one arm so hard it was rendered invisible.

NOAH. (*Turning pages.*) Here he is. Hugh Ignatius Daily, born 1847, died 1923.

OLD MAN. Man had a temper, though, ungodly temper, cursed his teammates well as the opposin' team, cursed everyone, God an' Man.

NOAH. I can identify with that.

OLD MAN. One one-armed man to another, right?

NOAH. *(Reading.)* "Hugh Ignatius Daily pitched a no-hitter for Cleveland against Philadelphia on September 13, 1883."

OLD MAN. Sonuvabitch! I bet Abner Doubleday was in attendance. Those were the Golden Years, Noah. The years before Relief Pitchers.

> *(Picks up a baseball.)*

So, whaddayuh say?

NOAH. Whadda I say 'bout what?

> *(The* OLD MAN *throws the ball to* NOAH.*)*

OLD MAN. Wanna throw a few balls?

NOAH. I don't think so.

OLD MAN. Don't be shy.

NOAH. I'm not shy.

> *(He throws the ball back to the* OLD MAN.*)*

OLD MAN. I'm just sayin'...

NOAH. I know what you're sayin'.

OLD MAN. I'm just sayin', humor an Old Man.

> *(Throws ball back to* NOAH.*)*

NOAH. I haven't thrown a ball in years.

OLD MAN. We'll drive out to Fairmount Park, throw a few balls. That's all, nothin' more, nothin' less.

NOAH. *(Fingering the ball.)* I don't know.

OLD MAN. Yuh got nothin' to lose, Noah, everything to gain.

NOAH. What will I gain?

OLD MAN. A place in my heart. A place in the Old Man's fuckin' heart. Whaddayuh say, Noah! A few balls, make an Old Man happy.

NOAH. Ahhh, Jesus...shit... Okay.

> *(*NOAH, *grasping the ball, takes a pitcher's stance.)*

OLD MAN. That a boy.

> *(Blackout.)*

Scene Three

(Later. The empty house. **COLMAN** *enters, drunk. He staggers across the living room, stops, calls out:)*

COLMAN. Hello! Hello! Anyone here?! Anyone home?! It's me, it's Tokie! *Tokie, Tokie, Tokie...* Back from the Wars, back from the Goddamn Trenches! Off an' runnin', though! Off an' fuckin' runnin' again! Now you see me, now you don't! Abracadabra!

(He crosses unsteadily to the bar, picks up the backpack.)

Where is he? Where's Tokie! I can't find him! Tokie's missing! Tokie's disappeared again! Fuckin' abracadabra!

(He downs a long shot of liquor, crosses the room, stops in front of the family photo.)

Whaddayuh say, Dad, Dale, Mom? How yuh doin'? How 'bout a kiss, Mom. It's been a while. How 'bout a big ol' moma's kiss!

(Picks up the photo.)

Don't mind if I take this along, d'ya? On the Boardwalk in Atlantic City. One good memory outta a million lousy ones!

(Shoves photo into his backpack.)

Any other memorabilia hanging 'round.

(Empties drawer onto the floor, items fall out: playing cards, chips, a small recorder...)

Nothing here, bunch a crap.

(He starts for the door. The recorder begins playing. A **WOMAN** *sings in an Irish accent.)*

WOMAN'S VOICE.
OVER IN KILLARNEY,
MANY YEARS AGO,
ME MITHER SANG A SONG TO ME
IN TONES SO SWEET AND LOW.

COLMAN. What the fuck! Mom!

MOTHER'S VOICE.
JUST A SIMPLE LITTLE DITTY,
IN HER GOOD OULD IRISH WAY...

COLMAN. *Shut up, Mom! Shut up! Don't wanna hear you!*

MOTHER'S VOICE.
...AND I'D GIVE THE WORLD IF SHE COULD SING
THAT SONG TO ME THIS DAY.

COLMAN. Leavin' us like that! Dyin' an leavin' us!

MOTHER'S VOICE.
TOO-RA-LOO-RA-LOO-RAL,
TOO-RA-LOO-RA-LI...

> (**COLMAN** *crushes the recorder with his foot. The music continues to play, louder now. The* **MOTHER'S VOICE** *resonates through the room.* **COLMAN** *covers his ears to drown out the sound. He stumbles to the bar, downs a long swig of liquor.)*

COLMAN. *Fuckin', Mom! Fuckin', Dad! Fuckin' Dale!*

> (*He crosses the room, unstable, falls, tries to stand, falls again.*)

Fucking family!

> (*He passes out. A long moment.* **LANE** *calls out from upstairs.*)

LANE. Noah...?! You there, Noah?! I pressed my ear against the safe and heard the clicks. There is no money or valuables inside, Noah, only stories, lots an' lots a stories. Noah?! Noah...?!

> (*Blackout.*)

Scene Four

(*Late afternoon. Rain, thunder, lightning.* **COLMAN** *on the floor, asleep.* **DALE** *crosses into the house, takes off his wet jacket.*)

DALE. *(Sees* **COLMAN**.*)* Colman.

(*Crosses over, pushes* **COLMAN** *with his foot.*)

Wake up, Colman!

COLMAN. *(Waking.)* Ahhh, Jesus. What time is it? What day is it? What year is it?

DALE. Tied one on, huh?

COLMAN. More like two or three.

(**DALE** *picks up the junk from the floor.* **COLMAN** *picks up his backpack.*)

DALE. You going somewhere, Colman?

COLMAN. 'Bout that time. Advise you to do the same, li'l brother.

DALE. I'm not going anywhere, Colman. This is my home.

COLMAN. This is not your home, Dale, this has never been your home, this is Dad's home.

DALE. I live here.

COLMAN. You don't live here, you exist here. Come with me.

DALE. An' what about Lane? You gonna leave her here? You just gonna walk out on her?

COLMAN. I made her no promises.

DALE. She's carrying your child!

COLMAN. She's carrying a lotta Hot Air is what she's carrying!

DALE. You're a sonuvabitch, Colman. You don't care 'bout nothin' or no one.

COLMAN. I care 'bout you, Dale. C'mon! Leave Fishtown. Gain a whole new perspective.

DALE. Don't need a whole new perspective. Happy with my old perspective.

COLMAN. You're burying your head in the sand again, Dale.

DALE. It's my head, Colman. I'll bury it wherever I please.

COLMAN. Noah's a madman! He hurts people! Warning you.

DALE. I'll take my chances.

COLMAN. You always been an obstinate sonuvabitch.

DALE. It takes one to know one.

COLMAN. Come with me, Dale. Let me make it up to you.

DALE. Case a Brotherly Love, huh?

COLMAN. Something like that. Whaddayuh say?

DALE. Too little, too late, Colman, sorry.

COLMAN. Ahhh, Jesus, Dale, what does it take...

DALE. It takes what you can't give, Colman. Never could give!

COLMAN. I'm trying to give you something right now, Dale. Take it!

DALE. I don't want it, Colman! Don't you understand! I don't want your shit! Go on! Get outta here!

COLMAN. *I'm trying to save your ass, Brother!*

DALE. I'll save my own ass!

COLMAN. You couldn't save a hair on your chinny chin chin!

> (*He turns to leave.* **DALE** *tackles him, knocking him down. They wrestle, fight. Front door opens.*)

OLD MAN. *Jesus and fuckin' Mary!*

> (*He and* **NOAH** *stand there, soaked to the skin.*)

Can't leave you boys alone for a minute.

> (*Crosses in.*)

Game called 'cause a rain, 'magine! Li'l sprinkle an' they're off an' runnin'! Something amazing happened, though, you tell 'em, Noah!

NOAH. No, not interested in tellin' 'em.

OLD MAN. Fella don't wanna blow his own horn so I'll blow it for him. Sky opened up in a Blaze a Glory is what happened. Stars were born, universes created...

NOAH. You're exaggerating.

OLD MAN. I never exaggerate. I may push the envelope a bit, but who doesn't.

COLMAN. What happened?

OLD MAN. Noah pitched eight perfect innings.

DALE. How is that possible?

OLD MAN. You see, right there, Little Minds, Little fuckin' Minds.

DALE. I don't have a Little Mind, Dad.

COLMAN. How could he pitch eight perfect innings, Dad. He only has one arm.

OLD MAN. How did God create the Heavens an' the Earth. He only had one arm.

COLMAN. C'mon, Dad...

OLD MAN. Who's to dispute me. Why must God be intact. It don't say in no Bible, old or new, that God is intact. They don't broach the subject. I'll go with a one-armed God.

COLMAN. Maybe he would've done a better job if he had two arms.

NOAH. He has a point there.

OLD MAN. The only point he has is the point at the top of his head.

COLMAN. That's real sweet, Dad.

OLD MAN. You lack an imagination, Colman.

COLMAN. I'm sure I lack a lotta things, Dad.

OLD MAN. That's the one thing I gotta say 'bout your brother, 'bout Dale. He's lacking in a lotta shit, daily shit, work a day living shit but he has an abundance of imagination.

DALE. That's the nicest thing you ever said about me, Dad.

OLD MAN. Well, don't let it go to your head, Dale.

(*Crosses to* **NOAH**.)

This young fella with his one arm can throw a ball faster than Feller or Koufax or even the Big Train himself, Walter Johnson.

NOAH. I surprised myself.

OLD MAN. I saw God today on that Ballfield. I felt his Holy presence in every pitch Noah threw.

(**LANE** *crosses downstairs.*)

NOAH. No one ever called me Holy before.

OLD MAN. I got down on my knees and I blessed the ground. This was no fuckin' hallucination, this was a miracle, honest to God, a one-armed man, a Freak of Nature...

LANE. Noah's no Freak. He was born with two arms.

OLD MAN. I stand corrected. Let's put it this way, you were endowed.

NOAH. I was endowed?

OLD MAN. God took away one arm but endowed the other arm with miraculous powers.

NOAH. God didn't take away my arm, a Butcher did.

DALE. A Butcher?

NOAH. We were starving, hadn't had so much as a crumb of bread in days. Lane was withering away, her bones protruding through her skin. Went to the corner Butcher Shop, slabs a meat hanging from hooks, grabbed a chunk, Butcher swung at my arm with his cleaver.

DALE. Oh, my God.

NOAH. Blood everywhere. On the meat, on me, on the customers. People were screaming. I stared down at my arm on the ground just before I passed out.

DALE. I thought you lost your arm in a car accident.

NOAH. That too is a possibility. The truth of the matter is I lost it. Who gives a shit.

OLD MAN. The truth of the matter is no one got on base today. Not one bat touched the ball. Gonna call the Philadelphia Phillies.

NOAH. That's not necessary.

OLD MAN. Well, who do you wanna call? The Yankees? The Cardinals? What's your pleasure?

NOAH. I don't wanna call no one. I don't wanna play ball.

OLD MAN. You don't wanna play what?

NOAH. Ball. Baseball. I have other fish to fry.

OLD MAN. What fuckin' fish! You can be a Major Leaguer! You can be one of the best!

NOAH. I'm not interested in baseball, Old Man, don'tcha get it! I went out there to humor you. I don't give a Peddler's fart for the Major Leagues! Fuck the Philadelphia Phillies! Fuck First Base an' Home Plate an' the Dug Out an' all the sweat an' commotion an' the Roar of the Crowd! Fuck baseball!

OLD MAN. Fuck baseball?

NOAH. Fuck fuckin' baseball!

OLD MAN. How dare you! How fuckin' dare you...say that... speak those words in this house...at this time...in my home...you ingrate...you worthless piece a one-armed shit! You Good for Nothing!

(*A long pause.*)

COLMAN. Dad...?

DALE. Pop...?

LANE. Noah?

NOAH. (*Controlling himself.*) It's okay.

OLD MAN. What did I do! What did I say!

LANE. You said it. You said those words.

NOAH. It's okay, Lane, really. I can handle it.

OLD MAN. I have no idea.

NOAH. I prefer it this way. I prefer the cards on the table.

OLD MAN. What's he talkin' about? What cards?

NOAH. Time to get down to business anyway. How'd you make out up there, Lane? Yuh crack that safe?

LANE. I opened the safe, Noah.

NOAH. You opened the safe?

DALE. What safe? Not my safe!

NOAH. What's in there? How much is in there?

LANE. There's no money in there, Noah. Just stories. Hundreds a stories.

DALE. You opened my safe?!

NOAH. *Sonuvabitch!*

LANE. Listened to the tumblers like you told me to, Noah, heard the clicks.

DALE. *Oh, God! Oh, my God! No, no...!*

> *(He runs around the room in a circle, bumping into things. He runs up the stairs.)*

NOAH. What's wrong with him. He got a weed up his ass!

> (**DALE** *appears upstairs, clutching manuscript pages, which drop on the stairs.)*

DALE. Someone's been in my safe! Someone's been reading my stories!

LANE. Not all of them, Dale, just three or four.

DALE. *Oh, God, Oh my God! No, no, no...*

> (**DALE** *on his knees on the floor, clutching the pages.* **LANE** *crosses to him.)*

LANE. It's okay, Dale, it's all right. They're wonderful stories. They're glorious stories.

DALE. What...?

LANE. I loved your stories.

DALE. You loved 'em?

LANE. Every word, every syllable, every punctuation mark.

DALE. *(Stunned.)* You loved my stories...

NOAH. 'Nough a this shit! Where's the money, Old Man! Where you hidin' the money!

OLD MAN. There is no money, Noah. What makes you think there's money?

NOAH. I smell the money, Old Man, I have a nose for it. This house stinks a cash!

OLD MAN. This house stinks of nickels an' dimes, Noah. The change from the Newsstand.

NOAH. I don't believe you! You're lying!

> *(The* **OLD MAN** *crosses to the change bag, picks it up, and turns it over. Change falls out.)*

NOAH. *Sonuvabitch!*

> *(He crosses over, kicks the change across the room.)*

Sonuvabitch!

> *(The* **OLD MAN** *crosses to the bar, picks up a liquor bottle.)*

OLD MAN. I'll fix you a drink, Noah. Ease the pain.

NOAH. Don't want no drink. Don't want nothin'. Splittin' headache!

> *(He sits on the floor, holds his head. The* **OLD MAN** *notices the backpack on the floor, picks it up.)*

OLD MAN. What's your backpack doing down here, Colman?

> *(He throws it across the room to* **COLMAN**.*)*

COLMAN. I like to keep it close at hand.

DALE. *"Liar, liar, house on fire."*

LANE. What's he sayin', Tokie?

NOAH. What he's sayin' is Tokie was runnin' out on us.

LANE. No!

OLD MAN. Is this true, Colman? Is he speaking the truth?

COLMAN. Yeah, I imagine he is, Dad. This is what I do, I run.

OLD MAN. You braggin' 'bout it, boy? You proud of the fact!

COLMAN. I'm neither proud or remorseful, Dad. It's just a Fact of Life.

OLD MAN. Running away again. Again and again and again!

COLMAN. When the going gets rough, I get going, Dad. Story of my Life.

OLD MAN. It's a fucked-up Story, boy!

COLMAN. It's my Story, Dad.

OLD MAN. It has no beginning, middle or end. It's inconsequential!

COLMAN. It's the best I could do under the circumstances.

OLD MAN. Ten years running, ten long fuckin' years! Who are you, boy?! Who the hell are you?!

COLMAN. What you see is what you get, Dad! This is me! This is who I am!

OLD MAN. This is not you! This'll never be you! I didn't raise you to run away from life. I raised you to stand straight and tall and Face the Music!

COLMAN. What music you referrin' to, Dad. I didn't hear no music in this house, all I heard was the sound of your voice, drowning out everyone an' everything, filling up every room, every inch a space until there was nowhere to go, nowhere to breathe, nowhere to hear one's own thoughts, to be someone, to be somebody. There was no oxygen in this house! You were consuming all the oxygen!

OLD MAN. I don't know what you're talking about. I was just breathing!

COLMAN. Me, me, me, me, every minute, every second of the day. It was all about the sound of your own voice. You never took an interest in any a us!

OLD MAN. I took an interest in you. I took an interest in all of you. This is a Bad Call!

COLMAN. This is not a Call, Dad. This is not Baseball! This is fuckin' Life! I'm leaving!

OLD MAN. *You're leaving, you're leaving!*

(Runs to the door, throws it open.)

That's right, Colman, run, boy, run, turn tail and run again! Run, run, run, that's all you ever do, till there's no place left to run, no place left to hide!

COLMAN. Plenty a places to hide, Dad, world filled with hidin' places.

(He picks up his backpack. NOAH punches him in the stomach. He falls to the floor.)

NOAH. That's not nice, Tokie, talkin' to your Old Man like that, Old Man who raised you an' loved yuh! I never had no Old Man like that. Show a li'l respect!

COLMAN. *(In pain.)* What is it you want, Noah...?

NOAH. You askin' me what I want?! You askin' me that after all I done for you, the sacrifices I made, the lessons I taught you, how to con, delude, wreak havoc...

COLMAN. I've given you two years, Noah.

> (**NOAH** *grabs him by the hair, pulls him across the room.*)

NOAH. Two years a drop in the bucket. You owe me five years, ten years, you owe me a fuckin' Millennium!

COLMAN. You don't own me, Noah!

NOAH. Skin an' bones, body an' soul!

OLD MAN. Stop it, Noah!

LANE. Leave him be, Noah. He don't love me anyway.

NOAH. This is not 'bout who he loves or don't love, Lane. This 'bout a debt needs to be paid. We're leavin', Lane, three a us like before.

LANE. It can't be like before, Noah, things have changed.

NOAH. Nothin's changed, Lane, same ol' miserable world it's always been.

LANE. I need to settle down now, Noah, build a nest, a baby's comin'.

NOAH. A baby's not comin', Lane, told yuh, stop deluding yourself.

LANE. A baby's comin', a boy child.

NOAH. *There is no fuckin' baby!*

> (**LANE**, *stunned, crosses away.*)

DALE. You can stay here, Lane, if you like. We have plenty of room. There's a crib in the basement from when we were small.

OLD MAN. Basement filled with baby stuff, Rattles, Teddy Bears, a Jack in the Box, never threw nothin' away. Was hopin', praying for some kinda miracle, baby boy, a grandson, I could love an' cherish the rest of my days.

LANE. That's so sweet of you.

NOAH. I don't believe this fuckin' shit!

LANE. I like this family, Noah. I feel comfortable here. Safe.

NOAH. Is it me, Lane? Is it something I did?

LANE. No, it's not you, Noah, it's nothing you did.

NOAH. I would've taken better care of you, if I hadn't lost my arm.

LANE. It wasn't your fault, Noah. It was an accident. You were a little boy.

NOAH. I was a little boy an' I was at the Zoo. I was at the Lion's Cage.

LANE. We were at the Lion's Cage.

NOAH. I reached in and poked the lion.

LANE. You didn't mean anything by it, it was just a child's prank.

NOAH. I meant something by it, Lane, I wanted to disturb the lion, I wanted to wake him up.

LANE. He was woke up, he was just lying there.

NOAH. He was lying there, but he was ignoring us. So I poked him again.

LANE. And I said, "Stop, Noah. Don't do that."

NOAH. But I didn't listen, I never listened. I reached in an' jabbed him one more time an' he didn't even budge. I didn't even know if he even knew I was there.

LANE. He knew you were there all right, he was just biding his time.

NOAH. An' so I reached in as far as I could and jabbed at him harder an' quick as a wink he turned and grabbed my arm in his jaw and bit it off.

DALE. Jesus!

NOAH. I had no arm just a shoulder with blood pouring out.

DALE. This is a terrible story, Noah.

OLD MAN. It's a made-up, fucked-up story.

DALE. Why would he make up that story?

OLD MAN. 'Cause he's a fuckin' psychopath, is why.

NOAH. Yeah, that's me, Old Man, you called it right this time.

LANE. You're no psychopath, Noah, you've taken a lotta Hard Knocks is all.

NOAH. An' after the three thousand an' fiftieth Knock, a man changes, Lane. A man becomes something else. Sorry for what I've become, my apologies to everyone, but we're going.

> (*He takes out his gun, points it at* **COLMAN**.)

C'mon, Tokie.

OLD MAN. Noah...

NOAH. Yeah.

OLD MAN. I'll give you the money.

NOAH. (*Motioning to the change.*) What money, Old Man, nickels an' dimes, don't make me laugh.

OLD MAN. Not nickels an' dimes, Noah, cash. Thousands a dollars in cash.

NOAH. Thousands a dollars! Where yuh gonna get it?

OLD MAN. I'll show you if you leave Colman alone.

NOAH. I'll leave him alone, Old Man, cross my heart an' shit like that. Now show me the money!

> (*The* **OLD MAN** *crosses to a section of the wall, grabs hold of a loose end of the wallpaper, pulls on it. Money cascades down from inside the wall. An avalanche of bills.*)

Jesus Christ!

OLD MAN. Socked it away every week, ten, twenty, thirty years a cash. An annuity, boys. For the two of you.

COLMAN. For the two of us, Pop? I don't understand.

OLD MAN. Nothing to understand. Wanted to leave something of myself behind. A piece of the Old Man.

DALE. I had no idea, Pop.

OLD MAN. No way you would've known. Hid it while you were asleep.

NOAH. How much is there?

OLD MAN. Tens of thousands, never counted.

> (**NOAH** *runs his hand through the bills.*)

NOAH. We struck it rich, Lane! We're one lovin' family again, you, me, an' Tokie. Let's go.

OLD MAN. Colman's staying here, Noah. You crossed your heart.

NOAH. Got no heart to cross, Old Man, sorry. I need Tokie to carry my bags.

(Waves gun.)

C'mon, Tokie!

OLD MAN. *Sonofabitch!*

(He charges at **NOAH**, *who strikes him over the head with the butt of his gun. The* **OLD MAN** *falls to the floor.)*

COLMAN. Dad...?!

DALE. Dad...?!

NOAH. Warned him!

OLD MAN. *(Moaning.)* Ohhh...

COLMAN. *(Crossing over.)* Dad...?

OLD MAN. Where are you, Colman, can't see you.

COLMAN. *(Kneeling.)* I'm right here, Dad, by your side.

OLD MAN. Vision's blurry.

(Grabs **COLMAN**.*)*

Made an x, Colman. Tore my heart out each time I made one.

COLMAN. Tore your heart out, Dad, don't understand.

OLD MAN. Missed you, boy. Missed you every second of every minute of every day.

COLMAN. You missed me, Pop...?

OLD MAN. Took courage to run, boy, takes even more courage to stay. You can do it though. You can do it.

COLMAN. I can do it...?

OLD MAN. Got faith in you. Always had, always will. Pushed yuh away, boy, pushed everyone away, even your sweet mom. More I needed her, the more I pushed. Got the King Midas touch, everything I touch, runs...

COLMAN. I'm not runnin' no more, Pop.

NOAH. That's right, Tokie, you're walkin', outta here, outta Fishtown.

COLMAN. *(Stands, faces him.)* I'm not leaving, Noah, sick of leaving, I'm staying.

NOAH. Sink or swim, survive or perish.

> *(Points gun.)*

Warning you!

LANE. Noah, listen...

NOAH. Not now, Lane, later.

LANE. *(In Irish accent.)*
> OVER IN KILLARNEY,
> MANY YEARS AGO,
> ME MITHER SANG A SONG TO ME
> IN TONES SO SWEET AND LOW.

COLMAN. That's Mom's song.

DALE. That's the song she sang to us when we were small.

> *(The **MOTHER'S VOICE** reverberates now along with **LANE**.)*

MOTHER'S VOICE.
> TOO-RA-LOO-RA-LOO-RAL,
> TOO-RA-LOO-RA-LI...

DALE. Mom...?

COLMAN. Mother...?

OLD MAN. Flo...?

MOTHER'S VOICE.
> TOO-RA-LOO-RA-LOO-RAL,
> HUSH NOW DON'T YOU CRY.

NOAH. Jesus Christ, it's just Lane, singing.

LANE. They know that, Noah.

NOAH. They know it?

LANE. It's just a memory. They're just feelings, Noah. This is a Family. This is what we missed.

NOAH. I didn't miss this shit, Lane. I don't want no part of this shit.

COLMAN. *(Crossing to **LANE**.)* Never meant to hurt you, Lane, sorry. Never been 'round long 'nough with anyone or anything to know how I feel, don't know what I have to do.

LANE. There's nothing you have to do, Tokie, just stand there.

COLMAN. Stand here?

>   (**LANE** *touches him on the cheek. He pulls away as if burned.*)

No...no...

LANE. It's okay, Tokie, don't be scared.

>   (*She touches his cheek again.*)

It's called love.

COLMAN. Love...?

>   (**LANE** *nods.* **COLMAN** *raises his hand tentatively, touches her face. They touch one another tenderly and then passionately.*)

NOAH. An' everyone lived Happily ever After, and the Prince rode 'way with the Princess an' when he kissed her she turned into a frog.

LANE. That's not how the story ends, Noah.

NOAH. That's how my story ends, Lane. Life is not a Fairy Tale. Life is hard and cruel.

LANE. I don't want hard an' cruel any longer, Noah.

NOAH. Whaddayuh sayin'?

LANE. I'm sayin' I wanna live in this house, in this place, with this family.

NOAH. An' what about us, Lane? What about our family?

LANE. It's nothing against our family, Noah. You're my brother. I love you.

NOAH. *You love me?! You love me?!*

>   (*Turns away in pain.*)

You don't love me!

LANE. I would've withered away and died in that terrible house with that terrible lady if you hadn't rescued me.

>   (*She moves toward* **NOAH.** *He pulls away.*)

NOAH. This hurts, Lane. This hurts more than you can imagine.

>   (*He starts for the door.*)

LANE. Where you going, Noah?!

NOAH. *(Walking blindly.)* Goin' somewhere, goin' anywhere, outta here.

LANE. *Noah!*

NOAH. I just wanted you to be happy, Lane, is all I ever wanted.

LANE. But I am happy.

NOAH. You are happy?

LANE. Yes, here, now, with Tokie in Fishtown.

> *(She crosses to **NOAH**, holds him. He struggles in her embrace. She grips him tightly, strokes him.)*

Dear Noah, sweet Noah, my Noah.

> *(**NOAH** stops struggling.)*

OLD MAN. Family together again, praise the Lord. Dale...?

DALE. Yes, Dad.

OLD MAN. Can't see you, boy, can hear you though. Say your words.

DALE. What words, Dad?

OLD MAN. You know what words, Dale, your words, your precious words. Let's hear 'em!

DALE. No...

OLD MAN. You can do it, boy, go on, say the words.

> *(**DALE** picks up the pages, drops them.)*

DALE. No, Dad, I can't, I won't...!

OLD MAN. You can! You will! Go on!

DALE. I don't know how, Dad!

OLD MAN. I'll help you, son, give you a runnin' start. "Once Upon a Time in a Kingdom by the Sea..."

DALE. Not the Sea, Dad, a Lake. It was a Lake.

OLD MAN. A Lake, whatever...go on...

> *(**DALE** begins to make up the story, slowly, tentatively.)*

DALE. "Once Upon a Time not so long ago there was a boy who grew up in a Small Village on the edge of a Great Lake."

OLD MAN. That's good, boy, that's a good beginning. "Once Upon a Time not so long ago there was a boy who grew up in a Small Village on the edge of a Great Lake..."

(**DALE** *speaks with more conviction:*)

DALE. "And there were Fish in this Lake, Fish of all sizes and shapes, Golden Fish and Silvery Fish and Ruby Red Fish the color of the Evening Sunset. And the boy would stand by the Lake and speak to these Fish and they would listen to him and hear what he had to say because this was a Magical Lake. An' the Fish loved the sound of the boy's voice even though they didn't understand what he was saying. And the boy tried to explain that there was a World beyond the Lake, just above the water they were swimming in. And the Fish listened and listened and heard his words but try as they would they couldn't comprehend that right above the Lake was an Ocean of Air and above this Ocean of Air were clouds and above the clouds was the Night Sky and the Light of a Million Stars and a Great Vast Wonderful Mysterious Universe."

(**LANE** *grasps her stomach, suddenly, cries out:*)

LANE. *Ohhh.*

NOAH. What is it, Lane? What's wrong?

LANE. It kicked, Noah. The baby kicked.

(**COLMAN** *and* **NOAH** *stare at* **LANE**. *The* **OLD MAN** *listens.* **DALE** *stands in the light as it grows brighter and brighter.*)

(*Blackout.*)

End of Play